It's About Time

Book 2.5

Floyd Hughes

Dedication

To Paityn, Mike, Kayla, Adam and Heather; and to Josie, Bill, Dana, Larry and Sharon. Thanks for all you do for others and for the kingdom. And to my niece for her creative inspiration.

BOOK 2.5

The Young Ones

Introduction

My name is Jayden Hernandez, and I'm nine years old, but I was eight when all this happened. And I know I haven't explained what happened yet, but you won't believe it when I do. My uncle Caden said to spit out everything that happened, and he would record it all and then write it down, so that's what I'm doing. He and my aunt Hayden—seriously, this name thing is confusing— both experienced what I experienced, and they think other people experienced it, too. I know more people have. I've seen them.

"What?" Okay, my aunt said to slow down and start from the beginning. "Like when I was born? Oh, that makes more sense."

So, a while back, my uncle and aunt came over to stay at our house for a few days. They did this from time to time since they lived in Pittsburgh and we lived near Washington, D.C. I usually get to hang out with them and do stuff when they visit.

But this time, my parents kept making me go into the family room in the basement to play.

"Okay, okay." My aunt said they didn't make me go into the basement; they asked me to go there to play. She also said none of you can see my air quotes, so I should stop using them.

One of the times that they asked me to go into the basement and play, I was coming back upstairs to get something to drink, and I heard them talking. My dad seemed kind of frustrated. He wasn't angry, but he raised his voice a little. I tiptoed into the kitchen and peeked around the corner from the kitchen to see what was going on.

"I don't know, Caden. You cannot expect us to believe a story like that," my dad said. "It's insane. If I told you this happened to me, you would think I was crazy."

My dad continued to talk, but as I looked at my aunt and uncle, I noticed something weird happening. My aunt kind of disappeared for a second. Like, she was there, then she wasn't, and then she was back again.

"Wait, what do you want now, Aunt Hayden? Sorry, I mean, yes, Auntie, what would you like to say? A what? A glitch. Who came up with the term glitch?"

Okay, my uncle said my aunt didn't disappear; she glitched. It has something to do with science and time travel and whatever. Anyway, as I was saying, I thought I wasn't seeing clearly, so I tried to sneak into the living room to get a better look. But when I took my next step, I wasn't in the living room anymore. I was standing in a huge forest. There were trees and bushes everywhere and...

"Aren't they kinda the same?"

Okay, my aunt said I was in a huge garden, not a forest. I saw trees covered with fruit, and I saw animals of all types walking around. I kept turning around, and everywhere I looked, I saw strange types of plants and animals I had never seen before. Here is the weird part, as if this wasn't already weird. I started walking towards this loud crunching sound I heard. I walked past a tree with huge almonds on it and saw what looked like a freaking brontosaurus chowing down on the top of a melon tree, and despite what my aunt says, freaking is not a curse word.

I told you that you wouldn't believe it, but this is for real, guys. And it gets weirder. I heard talking so I followed the voices. My uncle said we have to add a warning that children shouldn't follow strange voices they hear or talk to strangers. But I followed the voices. I mean, this wasn't a normal situation, right?

When I followed the voices, I found a woman talking to a snake. A freaking snake! She was naked and talking to a snake!

"Okay, okay, but freaking is not a curse word!"

Anyway, later, my aunt and uncle explained everything that had happened. The same thing had happened to them, and they each told stories about it.

My uncle had even written a few books about his experiences, and my aunt was working on a book about hers. But no one they spoke to about it believed it was true even though they didn't tell a whole lot of people. Uncle Cayden said that many of the people who read his books just thought they were geeky science fiction stories. But now, I get to share my story.

"Oh my gosh! Fine, you tell it then. Just don't change it or make it boring."

Chapter 1: Cayden, Hayden, and Jayden

My name is Caden Roscoe, and if you've heard or read any of my stories, then what you're about to read will make a lot more sense. What happened to my niece, Jayden, is true, and it happened to me and to my wife Hayden as well. Whilst my niece claimed our name thing is weird, it really isn't—well, maybe a little. When I met my wife, I tried to use the commonality in our names as a pickup line. It didn't quite work, but here we are. My wife's sister named Jayden in honor of Hayden. See, very simple, but yeah, maybe a little weird.

Jayden agreed that I could take over explaining what happened to her. And as I promised her, it is in her own words and not in her uncle's boring words. And yes, it was a struggle to leave that last sentence in, and yes, she used air quotes around the phrase her uncle's boring words. But just so we are all clear, these are her words.

Although Jayden said a lot of what happened to my wife and me was boring, once we explained to her that it was God doing it, Jayden understood how important it was to share what happened. God had already taken my wife and me on several of these journeys, each separately, through time. We each called them journeys because that is the only word that really fit.

"Like seriously, that's amazing. Like God was doing this, the real God?" Jayden asked when we explained it to her.

"Yes, the real God," I said.

Her parents were a part of this conversation because once Jayden came back from her journey she burst into the room where Hayden and I were explaining our journeys to Jayden's parents. Although she was overwhelmed and was speaking even faster than she normally does, I quickly understood what she was communicating. Whilst

Hayden and I were trying to explain our journeys to her parents, God took Jayden on a journey of her own. Now we know that was the first of many. And we now know she wasn't alone.

Chapter 2: God and Jayden's Parents

Jayden appeared in what we now know as the Garden of Eden. I know many of you are skeptical already, but please, believe me, keep reading. I was a little skeptical of her when she described what she had seen. It's not that I doubted my niece. I knew God was using the Holy Spirit to take me, my wife, and my niece, and now we know many others through time to experience significant pieces of biblical history.

But this was the Garden of Eden. Even though Jayden wasn't aware of it initially, I knew that's what she was describing. The rest of what she experienced on her journey will sound weird as well, as if we hadn't used the word weird enough already. It also might contradict much of what you know or were taught. And maybe that's why God took Jayden on this particular journey.

Jerome and Hannah, Jayden's parents, were both ex-military. When they left the military, they married and started their own company consulting with the government. They did not consider themselves extremely political or extremely religious, but all of that changed around the time they had Jayden.

Right about the time she was born, it seemed that every decision Jerome and Hannah made had either a religious or political impact. Their family, friends, and even their clients weighed the decisions her parents made through their own spiritual and political lens. Once Jayden was old enough to start school, it got even worse.

Jerome and Hannah were consistently at odds with things taught in Jayden's school. Whether public or private school, situations kept coming up that tried to force them to not just side with a political party or position or religious viewpoint but to go against an opposing political party, position, or religious viewpoint. Although they didn't hide their beliefs, they weren't big on demeaning and ridiculing the beliefs of others. But that's what the school systems wanted them to teach Jayden to do.

It might be difficult for some to imagine what it's like raising children in this environment if you don't have any children. Rather than teaching children truth, history, and math and educating them, schools were politicizing the school systems. School boards were no longer responsible for choosing curriculums and setting education standards. Instead, they were weaponized depending upon which political party was in power in the local government. Because that changed from election to election, what children were taught changed from election to election.

Imagine the history and scientific principles a child learned, changing based on whatever political party was in power. Although actual history didn't change and scientific principles stayed the same, what a child learned differed with every change in the political party of the people on the school boards. And it was impacting the children.

Children like Jayden became victims of the same political mayhem I described in my previous books. Perhaps that's why God took Jayden on this particular journey. Like most children her age, Jayden was hungry for truth, and that's what God showed her. And through her, that's what God revealed to her parents. And the truth God revealed was historically factual, something her parents previously believed was true. But now they knew it was true because of what Jayden and the others told them. Again, yes, there were others.

Chapter 3: Jayden and School

As I stated, Jayden appeared in what we now know as the Garden of Eden. I know most folks don't believe it existed, but this is where God took her. As I stated, I was hesitant to believe her at first, but she made it pretty clear by what she described that she appeared in the Garden of Eden.

She also made it pretty clear that she saw actual dinosaurs. I also found this hard to believe. But that's what she saw. Schools taught that dinosaurs and humankind existed millions of years apart. The same schools taught that there were discoveries of dinosaurs etched into walls and caves by man. It makes sense that the people who carved the pictures of dinosaurs into cave walls did so because they saw them and not because they excavated the bones.

Jayden is a huge fan of dinosaurs and dragons. She reads books about dragons and is familiar with a lot of the lore regarding them. Not long ago, she began asking me about dinosaurs and how they fit within the biblical timeline. That's what made me go back and look into the actual science.

In her classrooms, she would ask about dinosaurs whenever there was an inkling of the possibility of discussing them. She wasn't disruptive or anything, but she was pretty persistent. Her teachers didn't complain because her questions were extremely thought-provoking.

Well, let me rephrase that. Jayden's teachers didn't complain until she started talking about dinosaurs and the Bible. Some of her teachers got really upset when she asked about dinosaurs and the Bible. Others got upset when she provided rational answers to her own questions. But once she returned from her journey, it got even worse. She wasn't just asking and answering her own questions; she was providing rational details.

Her parents tried to intervene and explain that Jayden found some new material regarding dinosaurs. That seemed to appease the teachers until Jayden started explaining how dinosaurs were on Noah's Ark. Although Jayden didn't tell the teachers how she knew this, Jayden knew this because she was on Noah's Ark. And she wasn't the only one from our time who was on the Ark.

Chapter 4: Jayden and The Garden

But back to Jayden's journey. Although Jayden was rambling like crazy when she returned from her journey, she was much calmer than I was after my first journey. She ran straight to her dad, excited to tell him everything she had been through. But just like Hayden after her first journey, Jayden's thoughts and words were all over the place.

"And there was a freaking dinosaur. Like a real one," Jayden explained as she approached her dad.

Because of how time travel works, Jayden appeared in the same place she was when she disappeared, only a fraction of a second later. Once she realized she was back, Jayden began spitting out what happened as she burst into the room. Hayden and I caught some of what she was saying as she rushed past us, but her parents had no idea what was happening. They thought some sort of accident must have occurred downstairs where Jayden was playing.

After a few minutes of her trying to explain, I knew exactly what had happened to her. I knew she had experienced her first journey—that God had taken her through time. It took a while, but her parents finally believed her, and they believed me. They thought it unlikely that Jayden had just overheard us talking and was making this all up. She knew too many details about the Garden of Eden and Noah's Ark.

Jayden said that after she saw the woman and her husband eat from the piece of fruit, they tossed it aside. We had to keep reminding Jayden that the woman was Eve and the man was Adam. I don't blame her for not knowing; I blame her Sunday School teacher. I mean, this was basic Bible 101.

Jayden bent to pick up the discarded fruit as the man and woman walked away. The piece of fruit they discarded was a pomegranate. When we told her it was Adam and Eve she saw, it confused her because she had been taught they ate from an apple. She bent down to pick it up because it looked much brighter and juicier than any fruit she had ever seen. I asked Jayden what happened when she picked up the piece of fruit. When God took me on my journeys, there were certain things I could touch, but I didn't touch other things because I feared they might mess with the timeline.

And Jayden wants everyone to know that she asked me to stop 'geeking out' about time travel and get back to her story. Jayden told us that she didn't actually pick up the pomegranate. When she bent over to pick it up, she felt the weird swirl again in her stomach.

I reminded her that what she felt was the Holy Spirit moving her through space and time. She said she tried to lean against the tree in case she became sick or disoriented. Each time the Holy

Spirit moved her through time, it took some getting used to, as it did with me. When the Holy Spirit moved Hayden through time, she barely noticed it after the first time.

When Jayden went to lean against the tree, the tree was gone. She was no longer in the forest. She was on the deck of what she later found out was Noah's Ark. And although the tree was gone, she ended up leaning against another young girl from our time. A young girl named Paityn.

Chapter 5: Paityn and Her Parents

Although I didn't realize it then, I knew Paityn. Well, I didn't truly know her, but I had met her once. Her grandparents, Adam and Heather, were members of our congregation. They brought Paityn to a Sunday celebration when she was two or three years old. Now she was twelve years old.

Like everyone in the Pittsburgh area, Paityn grew up an avid sports fan. She grew up going to games with her family to watch the Steelers, the Penguins, and the Pirates. Once she was of age, she started cheerleading and playing sports.

Her parents, Mike and Kayla, owned a local appliance business. They had both worked there and worked their way up the chain. When the last COVID pandemic spread, the company was about to close. They used all their savings to buy the business to ensure the more than two dozen employees would continue to have jobs.

Mike and Kayla were both active in their local congregation and their community. They encouraged Paityn's sports involvement and volunteered with and contributed financially to all the local teams in the community—even the teams she didn't play on. But as happens with most children, Paityn's love of sports overtook her love of God. She still believed in God, but because of all of her other activities, she had little time to spend with God.

Once her parents saw this, they tried to inspire her to get involved in local Bible studies, youth groups, and other activities within their local congregation, but Paityn didn't see the need. Paityn's parents had multiple conversations with her about the importance and the need to spend time with God. Paityn said she understood, but nothing changed. Her parents regularly prayed about it because they didn't know what to do. But God did.

No one saw how far Paityn was drifting away from God. At such a young age, I don't think she even realized it. One night, her parents were waiting for her so they could all go to a Wednesday night Bible study at their local congregation. During the Bible study, parents would gather with other parents, and youth, like Paityn, would attend a youth-oriented Bible study. It was not a youth night with games and activities. Instead, it was a time when youth could ask questions about God and talk about stuff they were struggling with, whether at home or school. The lead pastor of the congregation led the youth discussions.

Kayla was tired of yelling for Paityn to come downstairs so they could leave. She knew Paityn was reluctant to go, but Mike insisted. Kayla was about to go upstairs and bang on Paityn's bedroom door when Paityn came stomping down the stairs.

"Is there a problem, young lady?" asked Mike, surprised by Paityn's attitude. He knew she was becoming distant, but he had never seen her act disrespectfully or defiantly.

"I'm not going to Bible study," Paityn said, crossing her arms as she glared at her parents.

Mike was surprised by her attitude. Although he worked long hours, he always made time for Paityn. Mike put her ahead of work and ensured he was at every game she played or cheered at. He was home for family dinners, which Kayla insisted on, and Mike ensured he and Paityn had daddy-daughter dates regularly. This attitude and rebellion of hers was brand new to him.

Although Kayla was also busy working in their family business, she spent more time with Paityn. Kayla grew up as an only child of busy working parents, and she often felt neglected and alone. Kayla tried to do everything possible to ensure Paityn never felt that way. The more time Kayla spent with Paityn recently, the more she noticed that Paityn was more disrespectful and defiant.

Paityn was also more reluctant to do what her mother asked her to do to help around the house. At first, Paityn would claim she forgot to do the tasks, which her mother thought was odd. But more recently, Paityn began refusing to do them, becoming more argumentative and defiant. Kayla scheduled a meeting with Paityn's teachers to see if they also noticed this change in her daughter. After the meeting, Kayla realized Paityn's teachers, or at least the things they were teaching Paityn, were the cause of the change.

The things they were teaching Paityn at school were well beyond the standard school curriculum. They even surpassed the previous decades' progressive agendas. They were teaching Paityn that she, at the young age of twelve, could live totally independent of any parental hierarchy. They were teaching her that she didn't need her parents and didn't have to obey them. They taught Paityn that her parents were merely there to ensure she had food and shelter. They also taught Paityn that she didn't need anyone, including God.

Chapter 6: God and America's Schools

I didn't know it then, but similar things were taught in school districts nationwide. It had become so intense in some school districts that children were removed from the homes of parents who resisted or spoke out about the teachings. Many cases were pending on a state or federal level, but the students were still separated from their parents while the cases were pending.

The division it caused rippled throughout the communities in which it happened. In some communities, law enforcement officers refused to remove children from their homes. In other communities, boycotts and violence broke out against officers trying to do their jobs by following the removal orders that the school districts made the local courts issue.

I didn't have school-age children, so I was oblivious to much of this until it made the federal news (yes, by this time, the news had been federalized). Both sides of the political social media had a field day when it did. The political separation amongst the nation grew even more prominent, and both the Republican Congregations and the Democrat Congregations, which had replaced most other religious denominations, were quick to take sides.

Although it seemed like it was just another political battle, the few remaining God-honoring Christians, who were part of Bible believing congregations, saw it for what it was: more spiritual warfare. Kayla didn't know this at the time, but although her heart was breaking because it seemed her baby girl was abandoning their family and God, God was about to draw Paityn closer to Him.

Chapter 7: Paityn and Her Journey

As Kayla stepped forward to address Paityn's defiant attitude, Paityn put her hands on her hips and took a deep breath. She was ready to go toe-to-toe with her parents just as her teachers had taught her. But as she exhaled that breath, her parents disappeared.

She was now standing outside in a clearing in what appeared to be a heavily wooded area. She heard what sounded like feet shuffling behind her, and when she turned toward the noise, she saw several lines of animals approaching her. She screamed and fell backward. She knew there wasn't time to get up and run. Although the animals were walking and not running, they were close enough that they would be on her in seconds. Instead of running, she did the only thing that came to mind. As the first few animals came within striking distance, she prayed.

As Paityn closed her eyes and prayed, she could still hear the animals approaching. She still heard their feet moving, but that was all she heard. She didn't hear any growling or any other animal sounds. She opened her eyes and saw the animals as they approached and filed past her as if she wasn't even there.

There were animals she had never seen before and ones she was pretty familiar with. At least, she thought she was. Some of the animals looked like dinosaurs that she had seen in the museums in Pittsburgh and in books, but they were much smaller, like baby dinosaurs.

The animals were slowly making a path around her as if she was there and in their way, but other than that, they didn't pay any attention to her at all. As she stood up, she noticed something else about the animals. All of the animals were relatively small, not just the ones that looked like baby dinosaurs, but all of the animals were small or were babies, or at least young. None of the animals were larger than a goat.

Paityn heard a voice in her head say, "They are all young." She thought it was her own thinking, but she knew it wasn't her voice. It was a voice she thought she recognized but one she hadn't heard or listened to in a long time.

To Paityn, it looked like the rows of animals stretched far back into the woods beyond where she could see. She turned and started walking in the direction that the animals were walking. They seemed to be following a predetermined path through the wooded area. To her, that didn't make sense. All of these different types of animals and dinosaurs—she was positive that is what they were—shouldn't be walking in lines together. It was like they were all headed to a concert or something.

As she followed them, she wondered what had happened to her parents. Were they somewhere close? Had they sent her here because of her attitude? She felt a weird stirring in her stomach. It was like air was twirling inside of her. She stopped walking and knelt in case she was going to be sick. When she looked up, she was no longer in the forest. Instead, she was at the bottom of a plank leading up to what looked like a giant wooden boat. The boat was almost as big as one of the cruise ships that Paityn had been on for a family vacation. The animals were all walking past an older man with a beard and walking up the plank.

The man wore what looked like a one-piece robe. He didn't have any shoes on, but he had a stick he was using to hold himself up. He yelled something to someone inside the boat that Paityn couldn't see. At first, Paityn couldn't understand what the man was saying, but as if by magic, she suddenly understood him.

"That is the last of the seven pairs of clean animals. Now will come one pair of every kind of unclean animal."

Paityn heard several voices yell things back from inside the ship. Although she thought they were yelling at each other in English, she couldn't understand it because the voices were shouting over one another. The man apparently understood what was being asked. He looked up into the sky and covered his eyes from the sunlight.

"Yes, and then our God will send seven pairs of every kind of bird, male and female, to keep their various kinds alive throughout the earth," the man yelled back to whoever was inside the ship.

Paityn thought this all seemed familiar but couldn't quite recall why. She seemed to recall either hearing or reading something about a boat and pairs of animals, but she couldn't remember any details or where she heard it. It definitely wasn't from school. Despite what her mother and father thought, Paityn excelled in all her academic classes.

Although her parents paid a lot of attention to her, Paityn still felt alone as an only child. Whilst she appreciated their attention, she wanted a sibling, another child, to whom she could relate. All her friends at school had siblings, either older or younger brothers or sisters, who they constantly complained about. However, in addition to their complaints, her friends often couldn't do things with Paityn because of things they did with their siblings. Sometimes, Paityn's friends wouldn't share things with her until they shared them with their siblings. Paityn's parents didn't know it, but Paityn had only embraced the radical teachings from her school because she was mad at her parents for not giving her a sibling. It was her way of getting back at them.

As the man watched the animals walk up the plank into the boat, Paityn tried to recall where she had heard or read about pairs of animals going into a boat. It wasn't school, and it wasn't home. Perhaps it was "Sunday School," she heard the voice inside of her say. Yes, Paityn thought. That must have been it. She had heard about it at Sunday School. It was something in the Bible that God did to preserve the life of the animals, just like the man said. The man was Noah, and the ship was Noah's Ark.

Paityn couldn't remember the whole account from the Bible. Later, when she and the other girls were sharing about their adventures, Paityn explained why she couldn't recall the details of Noah's account in the Bible. Although she and her parents attended a God-honoring biblically based congregation, the youth pastor had transferred from one of the political denominations. He taught the youth that the account of Noah was only a story, not actual history. He taught them that it was a tale told in the Bible to highlight God's dislike of evil in the world. Paityn and many other youths dismissed the account because they didn't believe it was true. Now Paityn and the other girls not only knew it was true, but they knew why.

Paityn felt the swirling in her stomach again. It wasn't bothering her, and she thought she was getting used to it. Before she could finish that thought, Paityn appeared on what she would later learn was the upper deck of Noah's Ark. She didn't have time to take in her surroundings because

another girl appeared directly in front of her and
then fell into her.

Chapter 8: God and Josie

Of the three girls God took on this journey, Josie was the oldest at fourteen. Josie was also the one who I couldn't understand why God took on this journey. Normally, if you can call God sending people and children back through time normal, God sent people back in time to increase their faith. It wasn't to show them any new revelation. Instead, at least from what we could tell, God sent people on these journeys through time to confirm the truths already revealed through His Word. This confirmation increased my faith and the faith of the many others who God sent back in time. Yes, there were so many others, but more on that later.

However, Josie had more faith than most adults. She was a committed Christ follower, who loved Jesus, but who was hesitant to talk about Jesus to others when an opportunity arose. She even cringed when her parents would ask waiters or waitresses if the family could pray for them before her family prayed for their meal.

Josie had Christian and non-Christian friends and treated each like family. But sometimes, she got so involved in spending time with her non-Christian friends that it caused her to miss spending time with her family. Josie made spending time with others and engaging in all her school activities a priority over her family. She definitely loved God, but she also loved spending time with her friends.

Josie was also very artistic. She played piano and drew amazing pictures of her friends and family on any scrap of paper she could find. To top it off, she was a straight-A student. Although I had only met Josie once, her grandparents, Larry and Sharon, were regular attendees of the congregation where I was pastor. Josie's parents, Bill and Dana, also attended but moved away a few months after I became the pastor. Josie's grandparents, parents, and now Josie and her older brother were all committed followers of Jesus Christ.

Although Josie didn't accept or believe the controversial teachings taught in her school, she didn't ridicule or criticize the students who did accept them. She also didn't question the teachings. Although she knew they were wrong, she thought it wasn't her problem. It wasn't until we heard her story that we knew why God sent her back with Jayden and Paityn. It wasn't to increase Josie's faith. It was so Josie could learn how to increase the faith of the others.

Chapter 9: God, Josie, and Noah's Ark

The transport back in time freaked Josie out a little bit, just like it freaked out Jayden and Paityn, just as it freaked out Hayden, me, and all the others. Josie appeared inside the Ark although she had no idea where she was. Before she was transported back in time, she sat in her room, reaching for her Bible to look up a verse she wanted to text a friend. Her friend had been wrestling with some of the teachings at their school. The teachings encouraged the students to rebel against their parents in order to express their individuality. At first, Josie had been reluctant to respond to her friend.

Josie had been pacing in her room for the past twenty minutes as her friend sent her text after text, looking for help. Josie finally responded to her friend's text messages. She told her friend she could express her individuality without rebelling against her parents. Josie wanted to tell her friend that God honored families and wanted families to stay together and respect one another. The text conversation was the perfect opportunity for Josie to start discussing how bad the world had become concerning God's morality. But Josie was afraid to start the discussion.

Josie remembered her pastor speaking about a time when the world had become extraordinarily evil and violent. The pastor said that every person on the planet at that time had engaged in violence against one another, including family members. Josie was trying to recall the passage in Scripture referenced by the pastor. She thought it was in Genesis and reached for her Bible to look it up. Josie thought if she could find the passage, she might find the courage to share it with her friend. At that exact moment, she felt a weird gurgling in her stomach, and then instantly, she was sitting on the floor of the lower level of the ark instead of her bed.

Although Noah's Ark is one of the most popular accounts from the Bible, it is also one of the most misunderstood. Many atheists and those who argue against Christianity argue that the flood shows God as a moral monster. Their claim is, why else would God flood the world and cause the deaths of so many innocent men, women, and children? Those who make that argument clearly haven't read the Bible.

Yes, God flooded the earth, but that's because, as the Bible says, the heart of every person on the planet at that time was wicked. The word used for wicked is a word that means evil in thought and intent. God clearly stated that the hearts and thoughts of every person on the planet were evil all the time. And before people claim that evil intent doesn't equate to action, God also stated that every person was corrupt and violent.

It may sound unreasonable, but at that time, there weren't eight billion people on the planet. Although no one knows for sure, there were likely less than fifty thousand people on earth then. And every person on the planet had evil thoughts and intentions and was living them out in violent ways. Men were violent and evil to women and children.

Just let that sink in for a minute. Women were violent and evil to other women and children. And yes, parents were teaching and educating their children to be violent and cruel to others. This was the cultural climate at the time, so far removed or corrupted from God's perspective of loving your neighbor as yourself.

The only person on the planet at that time who was living up to God's standard of morality and righteousness was Noah and possibly his family. When God took them on their journey, Jayden, Paityn, and Josie didn't fully understand this. It was only later, when we all met up, that they shared their stories, and we fit all the pieces together.

Chapter 10: God, Jayden, Paityn, and Josie

After Jayden rushed into the room and gushed about her journey to her parents, Hayden, and me, we talked about it for the next few weeks. We met up in person and had numerous video chats and calls. At Jayden's insistence and after intense prayer, we decided to look for Paityn and Josie. At the time, we didn't know who they were or what my connection to them was. We weren't sure how to begin, though. None of the adults wanted to be the ones to search out and stalk young girls online. Jayden came up with a creative solution.

"Why don't we let them come to us?" Jayden asked.

We were sitting in the meeting room of a local restaurant near her house having dinner. Whenever we had these discussions in public, we isolated ourselves to avoid people overhearing us and thinking we were crazy.

"How do you suggest we do that?" I asked.

"By publicizing what happened to us?" she responded. "It's about time people learned what God was doing."

We all got silent. That kind of defeated the purpose of why we were all meeting and discussing these things in private. I was about to remind Jayden of that, but she didn't give me the chance.

"Don't you think God wants us to tell others about Him? About what He's done? Don't you think it's about time we let people know?"

The silence continued. I had written books about my journeys, and Hayden was working on a book about hers. But those were books, and many people assumed the books were works of fiction. They didn't think it was real. I thought about sharing about my journeys at live talks in local congregations, but I didn't want to end up as a pastoral joke. I had several reasons for not going public and was about to voice them, but Jayden didn't give me a chance.

"Couldn't you talk about your journeys at a church or something?" Jayden said.

"No congregation would take me seriously," I said.

"Ours would," Hayden said. "They love you, they trust you, and they'd believe you."

Again, there was more silence. As the meal ended, we decided to take our journeys public. We would start with my congregation. I would share about my journeys on a Sunday morning and invite folks back later that evening for a question and answer session. If it went well, Hayden would also share about hers that evening. We decided to keep Jayden out of it for the time being.

We hoped that as we shared at more and more congregations and eventually had Jayden share about her journey, the news would somehow get back to Paityn and Josie. We knew this was an extreme long shot. Since Jayden and the girls didn't discuss where they were each from, we knew it was extremely unlikely that two girls from somewhere in America would hear about what we were doing and reach out to us.

Although everyone was optimistic, I wasn't so sure. What if the girls didn't want to share about their journeys? What if they had already tried to talk to their parents about what happened to them and their parents didn't believe them? What if they had tried to tell their friends or teachers and were made fun of or ridiculed or harassed? The cultural climate of our nation definitely wasn't kind to Christians.

Then I had another thought. What if Paityn and Josie weren't from America at all? Jayden said the other girls spoke perfect English, but what if they didn't speak English at all? What if the Holy Spirit had allowed them to understand one another just as He had allowed us to understand ancient languages on our journeys? All my questions made me think this was truly a God-sized task.

Chapter 11: God and My Congregational Talk

We didn't want to wait too long, so two weeks later, I shared my journeys with our congregation on a Sunday morning. We started the celebration like usual, praying for our community, nation, and one another. We continued with announcements and music, and instead of a sermon, I shared about the journeys God had taken me on. No one responded, not even an amen.

There were a lot of confused looks as I tried to condense everything so the Sunday Celebration could still end on time. I concluded by acknowledging that people probably had a lot of questions. I told them I would answer any questions and give more details that evening.

We always enjoyed a time of food and fellowship after the Sunday Celebration, and that day was no different. However, people kept asking questions about my journeys instead of small talk and catching up. I kept telling those who asked to come back that night for more details. No one seemed to think I was crazy or making it up, which was good. Everyone said they would come back that night to hear more and get their questions answered.

Jayden and her parents drove in for the weekend to see how things went. We all agreed it wasn't a disaster. We only hoped some of the congregation would come back that night to hear more details and to hear Hayden talk about what she had experienced when God sent her back in time. We were shocked at what we saw when we pulled into the parking lot that night. Let me rephrase that. We were in freaking awe. We could not park in the parking lot because there were cars in every spot, and people had parked on the grass along the parking lot and on both sides of the road.

Years ago, we removed the pews in the building and replaced them with rows of chairs.

After a few years, we replaced the rows of chairs with tables and chairs. We always had food before and during the celebration, and the tables and chairs prevented a lot of spills. They also made it easier for people to eat, take notes, and talk with one another. Jerome and Hannah were ahead of us, each holding hands with Jayden. They all stopped in the doorway, causing Hayden and me to bump into them.

We were all shocked as we stood in the doorway and looked around the room. There was no room left to stand. People were sitting in every chair at every table. There were small crowds of people standing around every table. There were way more people inside than could have arrived via the cars outside. It seemed like people had been bussed in to attend.

One of the deacons approached me excitedly but also with a hint of concern. "I arrived early because I brought some friends to hear you tonight, pastor. But there was a line around the building when I got here."

"I can see that," I said, still looking around the room in awe.

"Apparently," he continued, "someone watched the livestream and forwarded it to folks who kept forwarding it. It went, um…what's that word for video stuff? It went…" he paused for a second, trying to think of the phrase.

"It went viral," I said, finishing his sentence for him. "Because of the livestream, it went viral."

I was talking to the deacon but had locked eyes with Hayden. I could see she was concerned as well. I couldn't tell what Jayden's parents were thinking, but they each held one of Jayden's hands in a death grip. I was about to suggest canceling the talk to the deacon and my family. If word got out like this, there was no telling what the consequences would be. I made my way through the crowd to the stage and grabbed my lapel microphone from the podium. I didn't even bother putting it on. I just held the microphone up to my mouth and was about to speak when I froze.

My eyes were glued to the rear of the room where at least a dozen police officers had entered. My mind immediately raced back to the scene Hayden and I had witnessed of a politician at an event. The police arrested him before he could even speak. The police officers entered and cleared a path as a police officer I recognized walked calmly to the podium. It wasn't until I heard it over the speakers in the room that I realized I had said it out loud and into the microphone.

"Oh, crap."

Chapter 12: God and The Aber-ites

I turned the lapel mic off as the police officer approached. As he got closer to the stage, I recognized him. His parents, Larry and Sharon, were members of our congregation. I felt comfortable that if he had come to shut us down or to arrest anyone, he would do so respectfully because of his parents.

I put my hand over the lapel mic and leaned down to talk to him. I was pretty sure I turned it off after my outburst. I covered it anyway to ensure nothing else was unintentionally shared with everyone present.

"My apologies for any traffic issues outside, officer. We didn't expect this big of a turnout." For the life of me, I could not remember his first name. His last name was on his badge, but I hoped calling him by his first name would show respect and build familiarity.

"That's not why I'm here, pastor," he said. "You may not remember me, but my parents attend your congregation and..." he hesitated and looked around to see if anyone could hear him. Although the room had grown pretty silent when the police had walked in, now conversations were happening all around the room, likely about why they were here. He continued in a softer tone.

"My niece watches your livestream regularly because my parents, her grandparents, Larry and Sharon, are members here. They were out of town this morning and were texting with my niece as they watched your livestream from their hotel and as she watched from her house, and..." he took a deep breath before continuing, "and a lot of what you said this morning, the stuff that happened to you...well...she told her mom and me that it's pretty similar to some of the stuff she said happened to her a while back."

I almost dropped the microphone. "Wait, what?"

"Hold on, pastor, let me finish."

But I didn't let him finish. I stepped down from the stage in excitement. "Wait, is your niece's name…"

"Josie!" Jayden yelled at a girl walking down the aisle toward the police officer I was speaking with. The girl, Josie, was accompanied by four people and another police officer. I recognized the adults but didn't recognize Josie. The adults were Josie's parents, Bill and Dana, and her grandparents, Larry and Sharon.

Josie turned towards Jayden in surprise and yelled, "Jayden!"

At that exact moment, another girl climbed onto a table and yelled, "No way!"

Jayden and Josie turned towards the girl on the table, and they yelled, "Paityn!"

I couldn't believe what had just happened. In a matter of minutes, we went from possibly getting arrested to a reunion betwixt the other girls God had taken on a journey back in time with Jayden. As the girls ran to each other, I noticed people taking out their phones and SeeMe devices. Although we wanted our story to get out, we didn't want people to harass or mock the girls.

I motioned to the family at the table where Paityn had been sitting to come forward. I recognized two of the people as members of our congregation, Adam and Heather. They were Paityn's grandparents. Although I didn't recognize the other two, they all made their way toward the stage when I motioned.

"Listen, officer, perhaps we should all go somewhere and talk."

"Not yet," Hayden said as she took the lapel mic out of my hand. "We came here tonight for us to answer questions, for me to tell my story, and for God to do what we thought was impossible, to help us find these girls."

Hayden stepped up on stage as she clipped the lapel mic onto her shirt. Paityn's family had made their way to the stage as all three girls approached, still chatting and hugging one another repeatedly.

Hayden motioned to the girls as she continued, "God has done his part. Now it's time for us to do ours." She turned the mic on and addressed the crowd.

"For those who do not know me, my name is Hayden Roscoe. I'm Pastor Caden's wife. Many of you have heard about the miracle that God did with him. Now I want to share about the miracle God did with me."

She looked around the room and took a deep breath before she continued. "Look, I know some of you are hopeful that what we are saying is true. I also know many of you are extremely skeptical as well."

She looked at the girls hugging one another and their families hovering over them almost protectively. She smiled and continued. "So, if you are patient, I'll tell you my story, and then we'll answer any questions, and then...if there's time..."

she paused and looked at the girls, "you'll hear from others that God took back in time as well."

Chapter 13: The Aber-ites

When we left the church building that night, it was almost 11 p.m. There were so many questions after Hayden finished her talk that we spent hours answering them all. We didn't want anyone to think we were hiding or sugarcoating anything. It was Josie who suggested we have people open their Bibles and fact-check everything we were saying.

After the Q and A ended, Paityn suggested we all pray. Although some folks left once the Q and A portion of the evening ended, many stayed to pray. They prayed for and with us, and we all prayed for the congregations and communities in our nation and for our nation.

Even though it was late and we knew we needed to get the girls home, we all headed to a local restaurant to talk. Although only bars were open, one of the families at the Q and A session, who were members of our congregation, owned a local restaurant. The Wagner family was well-known in the community. They had owned their restaurant for twenty-five years and always used the restaurant and their resources to help folks in the community. Every Christmas morning, they would open their restaurant and offer free Christmas dinners to families and individuals.

They suggested we use their restaurant to spend time talking when they overheard us talking about, well, wanting to talk more about everything that had happened. They opened it, prepared coffee and tea, and brought us some soft drinks, juice, and snacks. They showed Hayden how to shut everything down, handed her the keys, and left. This act of random kindness and the response from those earlier this evening had us all in awe. And yes, I know I need to expand my vocabulary beyond the use of the words awe and crap, especially in front of the girls.

As we chatted and got more acquainted, we realized all of the "Aber-ites" were connected through our congregation. Aber-ites is a term that Hayden gave those of us who God sent back in time. It was a play on a Hebrew word for one who passed through, sometimes interpreted as traveled. She thought it was cute, and the term caught on quickly.

Jayden was our niece. Paityn was the granddaughter of Adam and Heather, two congregation members. Paityn had talked her parents, Mike and Kayla, into joining her and her grandparents to hear us speak. Paityn told her grandparents about her journey back in time immediately after it had happened. They, in turn, suggested that she tell her parents. Paityn was reluctant to do so, especially after realizing how wrong she had been in the way she had treated them. Her grandparents are the ones who suggested that Paityn show her parents the viral video and invite them to come to the Q and A.

Josie had told her parents and family about her experience almost daily since it had happened. She revealed some new aspect or detail she had forgotten each time she did. Her grandparents, Larry and Sharon, were also members of our congregation. They cut their trip short so they could be here tonight with Josie.

Her parents, Bill and Dana, had attended years ago but then moved away. Although her parents wanted to believe her, they just weren't sure. Josie wasn't one to make up stories, but this was a bit difficult for them to swallow. When they heard about it and saw the livestream, they planned to attend the Q and A.

Now we were all together. As the adults got acquainted and shared the stories leading up to this moment, the girls continued to talk, hug, laugh, cry, and pray. They were thrilled to have found each other. They were also extremely grateful to God.

Once we were all settled in with snacks and beverages, I wanted everyone's opinion about how everything went at the Q and A. I also wanted to discuss some of the questions people had asked. However, Jayden wanted to discuss what she, Paityn, and Josie had experienced. She wanted to talk about their journey. All of the parents agreed.

All the parents wanted clarity, confirmation, and answers to some of their questions.

After Hayden finished talking about her journey and what she had experienced when God took her back in time, there were so many questions that the girls didn't get to share about their journeys. Jayden made it clear that their story needed to be heard. For the record, she wants me to remind everyone that this is still her story. I'm just the "narrator." She also wants me to remind people that she reminded me of what I reminded her; no one can see my air quotes.

Chapter 14: The Girls and Noah's Ark

Jayden asked me to skip the whole explanation of a glitch, people disappearing as they are taken back in time and reappearing in the same place they left a microsecond later. We don't know if it's physically a microsecond. But we did ask an astrophysicist for clarity.

We didn't go into detail about why we were asking, but we are pretty sure he knew why. It took a while for him to get back to us, perhaps because he saw the viral video. When he got back to me, it was well after these events took place. And that's a story you'll hear about sooner than you probably think.

I agreed to skip details about the glitch even though it was crucial to understand what had happened to the girls. Even though it was late, we decided to hear from all the girls. The parents had already determined to keep the girls home from school the next day. What follows is me summarizing what each of the girls shared.

Josie was the first to appear on the ark. She appeared on the first level of the ark right inside the doors. She was freaked out and started to scream but stifled it by covering her mouth with both hands when she saw the open door of the ark and what looked like a parade of animals heading towards the ramp leading into the ark. She immediately began to realize where she was and what was happening.

I have to add here that her quick assessment and understanding of the situation stunned all the adults. When I went back in time, it took me a while to realize what was happening to me. Hayden had heard about my journeys, and it still took her a few minutes to understand what was happening when God sent her back in time. But Josie quickly realized where she was and who had sent her there.

As she turned and looked around at the cages, she kept saying, "It's God. God did this." Over and over, Josie repeated that along with, "I'm on Noah's Ark, and God did this."

All the cages were wooden and empty except for hay and water bowls. There were various sizes of cages, but none were huge. The largest cages could probably hold a small pony. Josie made her way to an area filled with wooden shelves, cubbies, and large tables. One of Noah's family filled all of the cabinets and cubbies with grains and leafy vegetables. The crates on the tables looked like planter boxes, and some had plants already growing out of them. Josie described the areas as larger than most grocery stores she had seen at home.

Thinking about the grocery stores back home made Josie pause for a minute and wonder how she would get home. Surely, if God had brought her here, He would ensure she got home. She heard a voice in her head say, "I will."

Again, Josie is extremely impressive. She immediately surmised that the voice had to be the Holy Spirit speaking to her. Although the Holy Spirit spoke directly to all the girls, Josie figured out it was the Holy Spirit speaking to them. She then figured out it must have been the Holy Spirit who moved them through space and time.

Josie's parents were beaming with pride when Josie told us this. Jayden and Paityn began hugging her and crying all over again after she shared that information with us, even though Josie had already shared this with the girls when they were on the ark. We could all see the bond God had built betwixt these girls. They not only shared a newly found love for God and His Word, but they also shared a unique love for one another.

Jayden cautioned me about getting too pastoral here, but I can't help it. The relationship betwixt the girls, and we later found out betwixt all the Aber-ites, is what the Church was meant to be like. It was meant to be people from different backgrounds, cultures, and life experiences coming together to worship God. It was meant to be people united by their love for God and His Word. It was meant to be what these girls were experiencing: the Holy Spirit-filled people of God united by their love for God and one another.

The girls were also united by what they experienced from their friends. They each tried to confide in one or two friends when they returned from their journey. They didn't go into detail, but they each tried to explain to their friends what had happened to them.

Josie had asked her friends if they believed time travel was possible. She didn't even get to the God part before they ridiculed her. Paityn simply asked her friends if they believed in God. Only a few said yes. The others threatened to report her to the school board for talking about God on school grounds. Paityn wanted to meet more frequently with the few friends who said they did believe in God. She wanted to spend time at their houses and hang out with them after school to ask them more questions about God. Eventually, it was the friends who said they believed in God who reported her to the school board.

Jayden asked her friends more specific questions. The same questions she was asking her teachers. She asked questions like why didn't anyone acknowledge that there were dinosaurs on Noah's Ark? Neither her friends nor her teachers wanted to hear any more from Jayden. They avoided her like the plague.

Josie made her way to a wooden ladder in the middle of the ark. Although I, Cayden, use the word ladder, Josie described it as a cross between a wooden ladder and makeshift stairs. She didn't need to use her hands to climb up, but it helped. It would probably also make it easier for people carrying any items and for folks riding on rough seas. She was about to explore the second level when she heard a loud outburst from the uppermost level. She was going to ignore it, but Josie thought whoever had made the outburst had said something about sandwiches. She was pretty sure neither sandwiches nor English existed yet, so she headed to the top level to investigate.

Chapter 15: The Girls and Noah's Ark Part II

Paityn appeared in the woods with the animals as they made their way to the Ark. She then appeared on the upper deck of the Ark. Paityn didn't fully understand what was happening until Josie filled her in on the biblical account of Noah and the Ark.

Jayden first appeared in the Garden of Eden. The other adults reacted the way I did when I first heard this. They asked out loud the same questions I thought in my head when Jayden told me, Hayden, and her parents. Didn't God forbid people from going there? Why would God take her there for only a few minutes? Would others actually believe she was in the real Garden of Eden?

I suggested God took her there first to get her attention. Her parents thought perhaps God took her there first to ensure God had our attention. We talked about this for quite a bit but didn't get anywhere. Jayden brought us back on topic by reminding us she was still telling us about her journey.

After the garden, Jayden appeared on the upper deck of the Ark right after Paityn. She was unsteady on her feet because of the swirling in her stomach and fell right into Paityn. Jayden was expecting to brace herself against a tree but instead fell into Paityn, which startled her even more.

"What in the ham sandwich!" yelled Jayden as she realized another person was with her. Paityn was also startled but was even more surprised by Jayden's outburst.

"Sandwiches?" asked Paityn.

"No!" yelled Jayden even louder. "What in the ham sandwich is going on? Why am I here? Why are you here, and where is here?" she yelled more than asked.

Paityn was speechless. She had no answers. She was still very confused by everything that was happening.

"Hello!" Jayden yelled. "What is happening?"

"I think..." Paityn paused and then walked towards a ledge of the Ark. She motioned for Jayden to follow her, but Jayden didn't move.

"I think we're on the boat from the Bible."

"Wait, what? That's not poss..." Jayden stopped short and pointed towards the sky. "What's that?"

Paityn looked up and saw a long row of birds flying towards the Ark. She looked over the side of the ledge and saw the animals that had walked past her making their way up the Ark plank.

"That's this," Paityn said again, motioning for Jayden to join her. Jayden slowly walked towards Paityn. As she walked, she kept looking from Paityn to the sky. When she joined Paityn at the ledge, she looked over and saw the rows of animals making their way up the plank. This all seemed familiar to her, but she couldn't recall why.

"Is this..." Jayden paused, trying to grasp the memory she couldn't quite recall. "This is like..."

"It's Noah's Ark," Josie said. Paityn and Jayden turned to see Josie standing in the doorway. "We are on Noah's Ark and..." Josie paused because she could see the look of disbelief on the faces of the other girls.

Although Paityn had suspected it, the reality of actually being on the Ark sunk in and frightened her. Wasn't that like in ancient times? Does that mean she was in ancient times? Were her parents somewhere in ancient times, too? She began to have a panic attack.

Jayden was confused and a little scared. The memories of the story of the Ark began flooding in as she realized what this meant. She was literally back in time—alone. Well, she was not alone, but without her parents or family. More fear began to creep in.

Josie began slowly approaching the other girls with her hands raised. She had seen this in movies and thought it was because it built trust, and she really wanted to build trust with these other girls. She was excited about this journey God had her on but was even more excited that she wasn't on it alone.

"Look," Josie said as she walked slowly towards the girls. "Let me just tell you what happened to me, and you tell me if it sounds familiar." Josie nodded and waited for the girls to do the same as she approached them.

Paityn and Jayden looked at each other repeatedly and slowly nodded. By this time, Josie was within arm's distance of the girls.

"Good," said Josie. "Here is what happened to me."

Chapter 16: The Girls and Noah's Ark Part III

The girls stood on the deck talking for a few minutes. As they did, the birds began landing all over the ark. The girls were initially afraid, but Jayden was intrigued because some of the birds that were landing were not just birds.

They couldn't identify them all, but some were small pterodactyls. Yes, stop and read that again. When the girls told us this, all the adults stopped them. There were a few minutes of silence as the adults tried to let what the girls said sink in. Although I was smiling after the girls shared this, I thought it best to be pastoral.

"Before the girls continue, let me share something," I said. "Right now, you are experiencing what has divided the Church, driven some people from the Church, and has plagued the mission of the Church from the beginning. You're experiencing doubt."

I continued before the parents could interject, "Yes, we all want to believe the girls. And we do believe much of what they said. It's hard to refute eyewitness testimony from girls who have only known each other briefly."

At this point, all the girls started to interrupt me, but their parents quieted them. They reluctantly let me continue. "But if we believe the girls about the other things, there's no reason to doubt them because what they are sharing now conflicts with existing theories."

Everyone was silent for a few seconds. The parents were confronted with evidence from reliable sources that conflicted with what they understood to be true. The conflict confused the adults.

Jayden wanted me to include the mountains of evidence that exists to show that man and dinosaurs lived at the same time, but I felt this wasn't the place for it. I probably should have included more details that the girls provided.

However, the parents and I were even more blown away by what the girls shared next.

When we finally allowed them to share whatever they were trying to interrupt me with, they all almost shouted the exact same thing. They hadn't known each other for a short time. They had known each other for a year. Jayden, Paityn, and Josie spent an entire year with Noah and his family on Noah's Ark.

Chapter 17: A Year In The Life

The parents began throwing a lot of questions at the girls, and yes, most of them came from me. All the questions centered on the same thing: How was that possible? How did the girls stay on the Ark for a year? Even though Hayden and I had been on journeys through time, we never sat down and contemplated how long we were gone. Let me rephrase that. We had never contemplated how much time we had spent back in time. We know we were only gone for an instant, but more on that later.

As the girls shared more of their experience, it turns out they really did spend an entire year on the Ark. Over the next few hours, they shared details, and we peppered them with questions. As Jayden pointed out, my questions were more of a commentary than actual questions.

We were still in the middle of questions when I suggested everyone go home, get breakfast, and rest. It was just after 5 a.m., and I was hungry and tired. As I stood up and stretched, I was about to ask if I could pray for everyone when Hayden interrupted me.

"I don't know about rest, but breakfast is handled."

"What do you mean?" I asked.

"Well, we're in a restaurant," she responded. "We're going to have breakfast here. That way, we can wrap up the conversation *whilst* we eat." I knew she emphasized the word whilst because I often use it, especially to make a point.

I was about to respond when Glenn and Stacey, the restaurant owners, walked in from the kitchen with plates of eggs, sausages, pancakes, and French toast. I froze. I didn't know they were still there. From the looks of everyone else, they didn't either.

Hayden saw the confusion and concern on everyone's faces and held up her hands. "They haven't been here the whole time. I texted them shortly after they left and asked if we could make breakfast here. They said they would come in and take care of it, and they did. They arrived thirty minutes ago through the kitchen entrance to avoid disturbing us."

We were still looking at one another in awe as the owners began setting plates of food on the tables around us. Although family-style dining had been outlawed a few pandemics ago, the owners felt it was okay since the restaurant wasn't open. When they finished setting up, I thanked them and asked them to join us. They declined. They prayed for the food and for us, and they left.

I turned to Hayden, but before I could utter a word, she said, "No. The Wagners threatened to leave the congregation for good if we even thought about paying them, tipping them, or reimbursing them in any way or fashion."

I raised my hand, but she stopped me by grabbing my hand before I could start an argument. "No," she said sternly. Then again, as she shook her head, but more softly this time, "No."

I was again overwhelmed by the outpouring of love and support we received. I was about to turn away as my eyes began tearing up, but there was no need. Everyone else had their heads down as they dabbed tears from their eyes.

"Okay then," I said as I stood up and reached for a plate. "What happened in that year?"

The adults started grabbing food. The girls remained seated and began excitedly telling us about all they experienced in the year they spent on Noah's Ark.

Chapter 18: A Year In The Life Part II

The girls were on the Ark as the animals entered and birds began landing on the upper deck. And yes, as Jayden keeps reminding me, some of those birds were pterodactyls and other forms of flying dinosaurs. Despite Jayden's objections, I won't go into a detailed list of all the dinosaurs on the Ark and the types of dinosaurs that flew. But she wants everyone to know she did have a list. Some of them she knew of before her journey. Others she came back and researched after her journey.

All the girls wanted me to emphasize the pterodactyls because they befriended one as you will soon see. Yes, read that again. What follows is a summary of our conversation over the next few hours until lunchtime when the owners returned and fed us all again. And Jayden didn't object to my adding the pastoral comment here of how much I love my Church family.

It took about seven days for all the animals to get on the Ark. During that time, the Holy Spirit kept moving the girls through time, day by day. They spent the majority of each day together and exploring the Ark together. They talked about the animals and began feeding them.

"Wait!" I yelled as I jumped up from the table. I bumped my plate, sending syrup and pieces of egg all over the table, but I didn't care. "You fed the animals? You were able to interact with the animals?"

It turns out the answer was yes and no. The girls put food into the animals' feeding bowls but didn't touch the animals. In fact, the animals seemed to ignore them even though the girls called to them and tried to get their attention. The thought of touching the animals didn't occur to the girls. Although the animals were all small because most of them were young, some of them were ones the girls had never seen before, so they didn't think of touching or petting them.

"Not even the cute ones?" Jayden's mom, Hannah, asked. "I mean, I can see not touching the smelly ones or even the baby dinosaurs, but what about the cute ones?"

"They were all adorable," Jayden responded, "especially the baby dinosaurs, and especially Jaxx."

"Yes," Paityn chimed in. "I miss Jaxx."

"Jaxx," Josie offered as she saw the confused look on the faces of all the parents, "is the Pterodactyl we, well, kind of adopted."

"That can't be true," Paityn's grandfather Adam stated. "I want to believe you girls, but surely you didn't really…"

"Did you touch him?" I interrupted. I gave Adam a halfhearted I'm sorry look for interrupting him. "Were you able to touch Jaxx?"

Hayden gave me a glance that meant I was being rude. It usually happened when I obsessed over a topic, usually something biblical or about superheroes. One time, she had to physically punch me in the arm because I was arguing with someone over why Green Lantern's power ring was more powerful than Thor's hammer. I was close to calling the person an idiot when she punched me in the arm, hard, twice. I have to admit I was obsessing over the science of time travel and whether or not the girls could interact with and physically touch living things in the past.

"Well, yes, we all touched Jaxx," Josie stated. "We touched him, fed him. He followed us around the Ark. I think he was the only one who could see us."

"But how is that...Ouch!!!" I screamed. Hayden had stabbed my hand with a knife. Well, she jabbed my hand with the blunt end of a butter knife, but it felt the same, kind of.

"Please continue girls," Hayden said through gritted teeth.

Once the door to the Ark closed, the girls started to panic a little. They didn't know how long they would be on the Ark. Josie was familiar with the biblical account and told the girls it would rain for forty days and forty nights, but none of them were familiar with what happened after that. And they weren't prepared for what God called rain.

Chapter 19: A Year In The Life Part III

The Bible references a ring of water hanging in the atmosphere at the time of the flood. It had been there since creation, but it all came splashing down during the flood. The girls described the loud crashing sound as if buckets of water came crashing down on the Ark. The girls were freaked out. Noah and his family were freaked out. The animals didn't even seem to notice. We've all seen videos of flash floods washing away cars, buildings, and entire villages. The girls described this as several times worse.

As the Ark started floating and moving, it started hitting things. Josie told the girls that the Ark was probably colliding with mountains and hillsides. Jayden suggested it was likely large homes, but Paityn voiced that it could also be bodies, large crowds of people caught up in the flooding. We watched as the girls again started hugging one another. None of us as adults could imagine what it must have been like for them. All they had was each other amidst one of the scariest times in human history.

The rain continued for forty days and nights. Paityn kept a precise count as the Holy Spirit moved the girls through time day after day after day. And every single day, throughout the day, the rains fell with the same intensity. Jayden described it as if God turned on the water faucets of heaven and then walked away and left them running on full blast for forty days. Then suddenly, the rains ceased.

Chapter 20: A Year
In The Life Part IV

A few days after the rains ceased, the girls went to the upper deck of the Ark. Josie thought it would be good for them to get outside again and get some fresh air. Jayden and Paityn were concerned they would see dead bodies floating around. Josie wasn't sure what they would see but thought they could all use the change of scenery. When they arrived on the upper deck, they saw nothing but water. It was like being in the middle of the ocean. There were no mountain tops, nothing floating, just water as far as the eye could see.

For the next five months, they appeared on the Ark day after day. Bill, Josie's father, asked if the girls got bored doing the same thing every day.

"Not at all," Josie replied. "We talked and chatted about Noah and his family and watched them interact with one another and the animals."

"But wasn't Noah's family bored?" Dana, Josie's mother, asked. "I mean, what did they do all day?"

"Same as us," Josie responded. "They spent most of the day taking care of the animals, and after they finished working, they spent the rest of their time together. They spent time together talking and laughing and being a family."

"And they prayed a lot," Jayden added. "We couldn't understand much of what they said but could understand every word when they prayed."

"And they thanked God a lot," Paityn said. Her voice got very soft, and she held back tears as she continued. "They prayed and thanked God for all they had, even though they had nothing but their family. We weren't thankful for ours, so God had to show us why we should...why we should..."

Josie and Jayden both rushed to Paityn and hugged her. None of the girls could speak. Once the tears cleared, Jayden told us each of the girls shared with each other about their lives leading up to their journey back in time. They each realized how ungrateful they had been to God and their families. They had each agreed that when they returned, they would never stop thanking God for their families, one another, and God's love for them.

They had also agreed to keep in touch but never thought to share where they lived with one another. The thought of exchanging phone numbers didn't even register with them since they had gotten so used to spending time with one another without smartphones or electronic devices. All the parents acknowledged that they hadn't seen the girls with an electronic device since they had returned. They also admitted they regularly saw the girls reading their Bibles and praying.

"Seems like God knew exactly what each of you needed," Hayden said. "He knew what each of your families, well, our family of Aber-ites, needed from each of you."

Chapter 21: A Year In The Life Part V

It was eight months before the girls were able to see mountain tops. A month later, Noah began thinking about sending the doves to seek dry land. When Jayden heard Noah discussing this with his sons, she became afraid.

The Holy Spirit only translated some of what Noah and his family said. Other things the girls picked up by hearing certain words associated with specific actions. Jayden thought Noah was going to send out birds, and she immediately became concerned about losing Jaxx.

"Don't worry," Josie reassured her. "Noah sends out doves, not pterodactyls."

Jayden believed her but was still concerned about Jaxx. She knew at some point his whole species would go extinct. She would have nothing to remind her of this time with Jaxx except memories.

"Sometimes that's all God gives us with the people we love," Paityn said. "Perhaps we should learn to make the best use of that time."

Josie told everyone in the restaurant that the concern for Jaxx led to the girls getting real about how they had treated their family and friends. They all agreed it had to be part of why God brought them to that specific time period. And that conversation seemed like an appropriate time for us to take another break. We spent the next thirty minutes or so hugging one another, loving on each other, and thanking God for bringing us all together. The tears of sadness and joy just kept coming.

It was late in the evening when Hayden stood up and said, "I hate to break this up, but are there any final questions before we all head home to some semblance of our normal lives?"

There were plenty. There were questions about why the girls didn't age and if they spent a year on the Ark, what their actual age was now. There were questions about whether or not the girls got hungry or thirsty. There were so many questions—some we figured out together, others we didn't. Life wasn't normal for any of us after that. How could it be after what we and the girls had experienced? That thought led me to a final question.

"I have one final question before we all return to our normal lives," I said.

"No. No more time travel questions," Hayden said. "We don't want to be here another twenty-four hours."

Others in the room muttered as they agreed with Hayden. And when I say others, I mean everyone in the room, including the girls.

"It's not about time travel, I promise. I just want to know the why."

Hayden knew where I was going with this and immediately sat back down. After each of our journeys, we debriefed but made sure to ask the why question. Why us? Why now? And what were we supposed to learn about God or ourselves from it? Although the third question asked what, Hayden and I titled this part of the debrief as the why.

Some of the adults were concerned that the girls needed to rest. They were discussing whether it was worthwhile to stay or to meet up at another time. But the girls had been talking as well. They all stood up, which got the attention of the adults.

"We'll stay," Josie said.

"And we'll share the why," Jayden said.

Josie and Jayden looked at Paityn, who was wiping tears out of her eyes. They both reached a hand towards Paityn to hold. Paityn briefly grabbed their hands and walked slowly over to her parents, Mike and Kayla. She hugged them both from behind their chairs.

"We'll stay," she said. "You deserve to hear the why and so much more."

Paityn's parents stood up and hugged her as tight as they could. The entire room broke out in another series of hugs and tears. It was another few minutes before Paityn interrupted everyone.

"Okay, okay," she said. "You know what happened when we were on the Ark. But a lot happened after we got home."

The girls each told us about their why, the reason God sent them on this particular journey. Although I was reluctant to, I shared much of it with the astrophysicist. Not right when we met, but after he and I returned from the journey God took us on.

EPILOGUE

BOOK 2.5

Paityn's Epilogue

When Paityn returned from her journey she appeared right back in front of her parents. Her parents were waiting for her explanation of her rebellious attitude and disrespect. They had no idea of the year that she had just endured.

Mike and Kayla were a little surprised when Paityn ran to her mom and hugged her. Tears were streaming from Paityn's face as she apologized profusely to her parents. Kayla was confused. A second ago, Paityn had been extremely defiant, and now she seemed genuinely remorseful for her actions. She seemed like the old Paityn to Kayla.

"Listen, young lady," Mike said, "I don't know what has gotten into you, but you are coming with us to Bible study. Period."

"Bible study!" Paityn yelled. "Absolutely, let's go. That's exactly what I need right now," she said as she grabbed her parents' hands and pulled them towards the door.

Mike and Kayla didn't understand why, but they saw a remarkable change in Paityn. She was more caring, responsive, and respectful to her parents. As Paityn sat in the restaurant with her parents, the other parents and grandparents, and the other Aber-ites, Paityn explained why.

During the year on the Ark, the girls indeed spent time with Noah and his family. They watched Noah and his family as they worked and argued. Some of the arguments were minor, such as what to have for dinner. It seems that particular argument is almost as old as time itself. However, some of the arguments were major regarding how to care for some of the animals that hurt themselves or why certain family members appeared to have easier chores.

Paityn noticed the argument about chores was mainly betwixt Noah's sons Ham and Japheth. Noah's other son, Shem, was always the peacemaker in those arguments. He would point out that nothing about what they were doing was easy and that they should each be grateful they still had each other.

He kept reiterating the importance of being together as a family. That struck a chord with Paityn. Although she had no siblings, she had a fantastic family of people who loved her more than she could imagine. Even when she treated them like enemies, they still loved her like family.

Over the course of the year, Paityn was privy to many of these arguments and disagreements. A few of them got so intense that it seemed like the family members would come to blows. But every night, there was the entire family—Noah and his wife, and Noah's sons and their wives—loving one another and taking care of each other.

"It's as if they knew that...at the end of the day, they were all they had," Paityn said. She wiped tears from her eyes as she continued. "And 'yinz' are all I have. And I am so sorry for how I treated you. Please...please..."

Paityn collapsed into tears on the table. Jayden and Josie were right by her side, holding her and hugging her. Mike and Kayla stood to rush to her side, but Josie held up her hand to stop them.

"Please," Josie said. "Let her finish. We discussed this on the Ark, and she really has to finish it."

Mike and Kayla reluctantly both nodded their heads yes. Neither of them wanted to see their little girl in such emotional pain, but they agreed to wait. Hearing Paityn use the term yinz, a Pittsburgh euphemism for you all or the plural form of you, made them aware of how important this must be to Paityn.

In the past, no pun intended, she used the term all the time, just as many Pittsburghers did. But once she started distancing herself from her parents, she stopped using the term and made sly remarks about them whenever they did. Mike and Kayla remained standing, wiping tears from their faces. To be honest, we were all wiping tears from our faces.

"Please...Please forgive me," Paityn continued as she wiped away her tears. "I was mean, disrespectful, and ungrateful. And, and I know I did wrong to you and to God."

Paityn tried to continue, but it took another minute before she could go on. She wiped her tears away, stood up, and approached her parents. Paityn took her mom's hand in one hand and her dad's hand in the other.

"I was angry over what I thought family should be, but," she paused as she choked back more tears, "God showed me what family really is, not what the school or friends say, but what God says. I know I acted wrong and don't deserve your love or forgiveness, but can you forgive me?"

Adam and Heather walked over and stood beside Mike and Kayla. Heather knelt and wiped away more of Paityn's tears.

"Oh, Ladybug," Heather said. "There is nothing you could ever do to make your parent or us stop loving you. And, of course, they forgive you because that's what family does, just like God did for us."

As Paityn and her parents and grandparents stood there embracing one another, we all wanted to join in and love on them. But the rest of us knew, maybe because of the Holy Spirit, that they needed this time together. Reluctantly, Adam and Heather removed themselves from the group embrace and left Paityn and her parents standing together, hugging one another.

After a few minutes, Paityn broke the silence in the room. She broke from her parents' embrace, walked over, and stood behind Josie.

"Alright, Josie," Paityn said as she hugged Josie from behind, "tell them your why."

Josie's Epilogue

Josie was silent for a few minutes. Each time it seemed like she was about to speak, she would get quiet again. Josie's mom, Dana, reached across the table and grabbed Josie's hands. Although they had never discussed it, Dana knew precisely what Josie had been struggling with.

"I should have helped you find your voice," Dana said. She squeezed Josie's hand. "I should have done more to help you find your voice."

"No," Josie said, "you did all you could and more. I'm the one who willingly refused to tell others about God."

Although Josie spent a reasonable amount of time studying God's word, she had been reluctant to tell others about God. That is, until she spent a year telling the girls about God's Word and listening to Noah tell his family about God's Word. Like Jayden and Paityn, Noah and his family had no idea what God had in store for them. Josie was vaguely familiar with the biblical account of Noah and his family. But each time Jayden or Paityn had a question that Josie couldn't answer from what she knew from the Bible, the Holy Spirit provided the information Josie needed to inform or comfort the girls. Josie imagined this is what God was doing for Noah as well.

A few weeks after the rains stopped, Noah's family began questioning why they were still on the Ark. The questions turned to arguments, and sometimes, they turned to yelling matches. However, Noah always encouraged his family to trust in God.

Noah would say things like, "God did not preserve us to see us perish." And, "Perhaps it takes time for that much rain to go away."

One time, Josie overheard Noah talking to his wife as they pulled leaves from some of the plants to feed the animals. "Our children continue to argue over why God still has us in here," Noah said.

"They argue for good reason," said Noah's wife. "God has not told us how long this journey will be. You and I have lived good lives. Our children are young and want to have children of their own."

Noah dropped all the leaves he had pulled into the baskets they would use to carry the leaves to the animals. He leaned over, kissed his wife on the cheek, and said, "The same God who knew when it was time to shut the doors to preserve us will know when it is time to open the doors for us."

"And you do not know when that will be, do you?" asked Noah's wife.

"Only God knows the day and the time," said Noah as he walked away. "Only God knows the day and the time."

Throughout their journey, Josie heard Noah continue to encourage his family. She often heard herself offering the same encouragement to the girls. Jayden and Paityn confirmed that neither would have made it through that time if Josie had not encouraged them, led them in prayer, and shared Bible verses with them. The Holy Spirit was with Josie as she comforted the girls on the Ark, and He was with her as she encouraged her friend when she returned to her room.

Right before God took Josie back in time, she was about to look up a passage of Scripture to text her friend. After Josie returned, she had dozens of things running through her head that she wanted to do. She wanted to tell her parents what had happened. Although Josie wasn't sure they would believe her, she needed to tell them anyway. She also wanted to tell her grandparents. She thought they had mentioned that the pastor of their congregation wrote a book about stuff like this. She wondered how she had even remembered that.

She heard the Holy Spirit say, "You have a copy of that book."

"I have a copy of that book," Josie exclaimed out loud, although no one else was in her room.

She found the book and then wrote a list of things she wanted to do and people she wanted to tell about her journey. Halfway through writing the list, she remembered what she had been doing before her journey started. She grabbed her phone off of her desk and called her friend.

"Hey, do you want to meet up really quick? I think I have some Bible verses that will help with what you're dealing with."

Josie wasn't in tears as she told us this, but she was pretty emotional. She sat silent for a minute and then took a deep breath. But before she could continue, I felt the need to speak up.

"Wait a minute," I interrupted Josie. "You read my book?"

"Seriously!" Hayden almost shouted. "Are you for real asking about book sales right now?"

Although Hayden was 100 percent serious, the whole room erupted in laughter. It was just the emotional change everyone in the room needed. Despite the laughing, Hayden continued to glare at me.

"I let a lot of people down by not sharing God's truth with them," Josie continued. "So many people who the truth from God's word could have helped...but I choose to be silent, just so no one would dislike me."

"But you have done so much for so many people since you've returned," Bill, Dana's father, said. "Between Bible studies and helping your friends work through their issues, you've done more than most pastors."

Hayden knew I was about to interject and elbowed me in the side. I wasn't going to complain about what Bill said. I was actually going to encourage Josie because most of what Bill said was true. Because of the state of many congregations and the almost explicit ban on talking about anything Christian, many pastors did nothing more than preach on Sundays. And most of those sermons lacked any biblical truth.

"The Church needs people like you, Josie," I said. "The Church needs people to speak the truth of God's Word into the lives of the people in their circles of influence."

I stood up, and Hayden sighed loudly. She knew I was about to go into sermon mode. I held up both hands towards her in a praying motion, meaning I was asking her to give me some grace.

"The Church was intended to be the people of God called into public assembly so they could be equipped to go share the Gospel with folks who don't know God." I slowly sat back down and motioned towards Josie. "Thank you for being the Church," I said. "We need you now more than ever."

I looked at all the girls and continued, "We need all of you to share what God is doing in your lives."

"Including this," Jayden said enthusiastically.

"Well...maybe not this," Hannah, Jayden's mother, said. "At least not yet, right? We don't want the girls exposed to, well, the crazies out there, do we?" She looked around the room at the other adults.

"But we can write a book with our stories just like Uncle Caden did and like Aunt Hayden is doing."

"I think that's a great idea," I responded. Apparently, I should have checked with the other adults first because none of them looked as if they thought it was a good idea.

"Hear me out," I said. "We can use fake names and—"

"No," Josie said, "I refuse to hide what God is doing. I will never hide from sharing about God again. If we tell our stories, it has to be clear it is our stories."

The room got silent as the parents contemplated what that meant. What the girls experienced would be known in their communities, schools, and their parents' workplaces. Now it was the girls' turn to encourage each of their families. As the parents started talking amongst each of their family units, Jayden stood up from her chair.

"God took us on journeys, brought us back to our time, and then brought us all together. He did that for a reason," she said. "Don't you think He wants people to know what He's done?"

It was the same reasoning she had used to get us to do the viral livestream that had brought us all together. I didn't know how the other parents felt, but I knew she was right. We couldn't hide this any longer.

Only one day had passed, a really long one, though, since the video went viral. What if more people were looking for us because they wanted to share about journeys God took them on? What about the people who didn't see the video but might read the books and then look for us? I didn't know what the other adults were thinking, but I knew Jayden was right. We needed to use every resource available to get the stories of the girls out there.

Every parent agreed to let the girls write about their journey. We all agreed it would be one book about their journeys. The girls decided Jayden could be the narrator, telling all of their stories.

"Can I talk about my journey with Jaxx, too, or just this journey?" Jayden asked.

"You had a separate journey with Jaxx?" Jerome, Jayden's dad, asked. "The pterodactyl? You had a journey with the pterodactyl?"

"You didn't tell us about that," Josie said, surprised.

"I didn't have a chance. It happened on our last day on the Ark, right when we left," Jayden responded. "I guess you and Paityn were taken home, but God took me to spend time with Jaxx."

Jayden's Epilogue

After more than a year, the door to the Ark finally opened. Although the girls wanted to leave the Ark immediately and run around on dry land, they instead watched as Noah and his family ensured all the animals safely left the Ark.

The girls' last conversation on the Ark was about how to get home. As they continued watching the animals leave the Ark, Josie suggested they do the same. Once again, she encouraged the girls that the same God who brought them together would take them home. Once the animals were off the Ark, the girls held hands and walked down the plank. As they did, they each felt a familiar swirling in their stomach. Paityn and Josie were returned to their homes about a millisecond after leaving. But Jayden appeared on a mountaintop.

Jayden looked around, but none of the surroundings were familiar to her. She was intrigued by the trees and the vegetation. For some reason, it did not look as vibrant to her as the trees in the Garden of Eden. Although she was confused, she had learned enough from Josie to trust that God had brought her to this mountaintop for a reason. She heard a noise behind her and turned to see Jaxx land on the side of a cliff behind her.

"Jaxx," Jayden yelled excitedly. "How did you get here? And where is here? And when is here?" she said, noticing Jaxx was quite a bit bigger than when she saw him moments ago on the Ark.

As if in response to her question, Jaxx flew off the cliff's side and began circling. Jayden made her way to the side of the cliff and carefully looked over the side. She was a few hundred feet up from a small village. There were maybe a dozen or so people in the village. At this height, it was hard for Jayden to tell which ones were adults and which were children. She wasn't sure, but this had to be at least a few decades after she left the Ark.

While she was looking at the village, she felt the familiar swirl in her stomach again. Jayden looked up to wave goodbye to Jaxx as she thought she was going home. Instead, she stayed right there in that spot. But instead of Jaxx, there were now Jaxx and a few smaller pterodactyls flying above her. She was excited because she knew Jaxx now had a family. She looked down at the village, and now there were a whole lot more people in the village along with more animals and buildings.

She felt the swirl in her stomach again, but this time, she appeared higher up on the same mountain. She saw Jaxx lying on the ground, not moving. He was about the same size as the last time; each of his wings was almost ten feet long. His eyes were open, but he wasn't moving. Jayden knew that Jaxx had aged.

"Oh, Jaxx," she said as she rushed to his side. "My poor little overgrown Jaxx."

Jaxx's head and body were too heavy for Jayden to move, so she knelt next to him. She sat with him and rubbed his neck like she used to do on the Ark. Jayden told us that God allowed her to stay there until right before Jaxx passed away.

"God must have known how concerned I was about Jaxx," Jayden told us. "So, He took me to see that Jaxx was okay."

Both Paityn and Josie reached over and hugged Jayden. The room remained silent for a few minutes more. The truth of what Jayden shared wasn't lost on any of the adults. If we hadn't been thinking about it before, we were definitely thinking about it now. Dinosaurs and humanity existed together historically. They did until, like so many species, they died out. Although there exists compelling evidence to support the fact that they lived together, nothing was more convincing than someone watching it happen.

Whilst the girls continued to comfort one another, the parents all had the same look of concern. If talking about God taking people back in time wasn't bad enough, now we would be calling the entire scientific community liars. Despite the concerned looks, we all shared the same thought.

It was the same thought Josie had shared earlier. We refused to hide what God was doing.

PROLOGUE

BOOK 3 and

BOOK 4

BOOK

THREE

Prologue: God and Hayden

After my first series of journeys, Hayden and I had a detailed conversation about all of them. We were at the kitchen table where we usually held these debriefings. That is what she started calling these discussions about my journeys back in time. She came up with that name after my journey to the time of King David's reign. She thought that since we gave the journeys themselves a title, our discussions after each journey also deserved a title. But after this debriefing and grilling, I was done, which is what I told her, well, yelled at her.

"Okay, I'm done!" I yelled as I got up from the table. "You don't have to believe me but don't freaking ridicule me."

"Wait, what?" she asked, unsure why I was suddenly angry and defensive. "I'm just asking the same questions that anyone…"

"I'm done!" I yelled, went into the bedroom, and slammed the door.

She was asking the same questions anyone would ask, but she wasn't anyone. She was my wife, my best friend, my confidant. She was supposed to support and believe me even if no one else did. But the more I thought about it, the more I could see her side. Over and over again, I had come to her with these miraculous experiences of biblical proportions. I had to wonder why she believed me. I mean, it was just my word. And her questions were logical ones, even if they were laced with her usual sense of sarcasm.

I was drained and knew I owed her an apology, but I wasn't in the mood right now. I was still angry and still spent. I lay down with the intent of taking a short nap. I picked up my phone and texted Hayden: *I'm sorry. I overreacted. I'll feel better after a nap.*

She texted back: *It's only three p.m., but if a nap is what you need to continue telling me about this journey, have at it. But I do expect a verbal apology when you wake up.*

I lay down for what I thought was a few minutes, but it was several hours. I was awakened by Hayden slapping and shaking me whilst screaming at me. I don't wake up well when startled, and this was more than being startled. I pushed her away and rolled off the bed into her, sending both of us tumbling onto the floor. She was still yelling as I tried to figure out what was happening. I was trying to stand but was still half asleep, so I kept stumbling. As I did, I was trying to hold onto her for balance.

"What, what, what?" I mumbled, wiping the sleep from my eyes as I looked around the room. I thought maybe there was an intruder or the house was on fire. Hayden kept yelling something the entire time, but I couldn't make it out.

Hayden quickly stood on her feet and grabbed the front of my shirt with both hands. She yanked me upward until I was standing, and then she pushed me backward against the closet door and yelled, "Listen to me!"

I shook my head, trying to focus. I was trying to look past her at the clock to see what time it was, but she grabbed my face with one hand and turned it back until I was looking directly at her.

"It happened! It happened! It happened!" she kept yelling.

That is what she had been yelling the whole time, but only now did I understand what she was saying. As I focused on her, I could see tears in her eyes. I began to get angry, thinking someone had hurt her. But she softened her voice and cleared her throat.

"Listen to me," she said more calmly this time. She took a deep breath and repeated, "It happened."

I stared at her, trying to figure out what had happened. I could see from her face that the tears weren't from physical pain. Her face softened until she was smiling. She put her other hand on my face and kissed me. She clasped her hands together and took a step back. She took a few deep breaths to steady herself.

I was still confused but began to relax, realizing we weren't in danger. I glanced at the clock on the nightstand next to the bed and saw it was now three a.m. I hadn't realized I had slept that long. Perhaps Hayden woke me up because she was tired of waiting for her apology. But that wouldn't warrant the slapping and shaking she had used to wake me up.

I looked back at Hayden, who was still taking deep breaths. She took a few more steps back and sat down on the side of the bed. This time, as she spoke, she wasn't yelling, but her voice was very shaky.

"Okay," she said, "this is going to sound weird, but it happened. It actually happ…" but she didn't finish the sentence.

She didn't finish the sentence because she glitched. She glitched! Even though it was three in the morning, and I was half asleep and had just been startled out of bed, I was 100 percent sure she glitched. Even after the glitch, she didn't finish the sentence. She just stared at me. We were both silent for a few seconds.

"Oh, crap," I said softly as I sank to the floor. "Oh, crap. Oh, crap. Oh, crap."

And yes, I'm a pastor who has literally been in the presence of God, who God has taken through time to experience His truth, who knows beyond a shadow of a doubt with unwavering certainty that God exists and that He calls His people to uphold His level of holiness, but we're just going to pretend I said, "Oh, crap."

Hayden and I sat at the kitchen table as she walked me through her journeys. It was now seven a.m., and she had been talking nonstop for several hours. It took a while for her to calm down and start telling me what happened because she'd spent about an hour apologizing for not fully believing me. She said she did believe me, but her belief was an act of faith. It's more like she believed me because she believed in me.

Once she calmed down, I walked her through some breathing exercises and relaxation techniques I had learned to use after my journeys. I told her that right now, she was excited, but once that went away, she would be hit with a wall of physical and mental exhaustion. We went to the kitchen, what I had dubbed the debriefing room, and she began to tell me everything as she made us coffee. Caffeine was the last thing I thought she needed, but this didn't seem like the time to tell her that.

But Hayden had definitely glitched. God had taken her through time to experience some of what I had experienced. Well, it was a few different experiences. God had taken her to other times in history than I had visited. As we talked, we discovered that in a short period of time (no pun intended), God had taken her on multiple journeys. She had been on two, seemingly back-to-back when she came to wake me up. It was whilst she was trying to wake me up that I saw her glitch, and God took her on a third journey.

I handed her another cup of coffee. She began to tell me more of what she had experienced as I bombarded her with questions. My questions weren't like hers had been to me. Her questions had always been to help her understand or to help her believe what I was saying. My questions were more about our shared experience and how she felt about what God had done to us, well, what God had done for us.

Hayden tried to answer my questions as best as she could, but she also wanted to get everything out, to share the experience of what had happened whilst it was all still fresh. But she had three experiences almost all at once. Mine were spread out over time (again, no pun intended). So, as she spoke, she would randomly jump between experiences.

I looked over at the clock on the stove and saw it was seven in the morning. I put up my hands to indicate we needed to stop.

"Wait, wait, wait," I said. "I think we need to take a break here."

"No, no, we don't," she replied. "I'm not tired."

"That may be true, but you need to start over. We need to record your experiences like we did mine."

She hesitated as she thought about it, and then her shoulders suddenly slumped. "That could take quite a while."

She looked over at the clock and then back at me. We both looked at her phone sitting on the table. I got up to make breakfast as she grabbed her phone and called her work.

"Hi, yes, this is Hayden. I think I'm going to need to take the day off."

I tossed a spoon onto the table, which caused her to look up at me. I gave her a stern look and tried to signal with my hands that we would need more time. She looked confused at first but then caught on.

"I meant take the week off," she said. I was about to sit at the table but paused when I heard her say week. She looked at me and nodded as she continued her conversation.

"A whole week!" I exclaimed when she got off the phone. "Seriously? One whole week?"

"Trust me," she said, "even that may not be enough time." She purposefully emphasized the word time and winked at me as she said it.

I had been doing this with her since God took me on my first journey. I would joke about time or use the word time in a funny way and either wink at her or elbow her to make sure she got the pun.

I sat down and slid a bowl of cereal across to her. I grabbed an old smartphone we had been using to record me talking about my journeys. The voice recorder function was much easier than writing it all down.

"Remember, start at the beginning," I said as I pressed the record button, then slid the phone across the table to her.

"My name is Hayden Roscoe, and if you have ever read the book of Esther or heard of Queen Esther, you will want to hear what I have to say."

BOOK

FOUR

Prologue: Here We Go

About six months had passed since the video went viral. Those six months allowed the initial interest to die down. After the first several weeks, attendance at the Sunday Celebration increased dramatically, then slowly died down. We expected that. Sales of my books about my experience continued to rise, though. Apparently, folks who would never step foot into one of our Sunday Celebrations were interested in what I had to say. They just didn't want to hear it in person. We expected that as well.

What we didn't expect was the amount of hate and screams of "fake pastor" and "false prophet" we would receive online. We expected some pushback, but not at this level. We also didn't expect so many hateful comments from people in our community who knew us. We also didn't expect most of those to come from pastors who knew me. I was so grateful we didn't let the girls share their story that night. None of them deserved to go through the hate and anger we were experiencing.

Hayden suggested that some people who knew us might have felt betrayed or lied to by my story. She also thought some of the pastors thought I was using theatrics to get their people to attend our Sunday Celebrations and to sell books. Many of the initial influx of attendees at our Sunday Celebration came from other pastors' congregations.

Over time, things died down, but Hayden, the girls, and I continued to get together regularly—sometimes with their families and sometimes only Hayden and the girls. Once the summer hit, Jayden spent the entire summer with us to be near Paityn and Josie.

The girls got together every single day or would spend days at a time at our house or Josie's or Paityn's house. Some days, they would do girl stuff and summer stuff, hanging out together and enjoying the summer, but they started and ended every day giving thanks to God.

It was about that time that the astrophysicist finally got back to me. The astrophysicist asked me to keep his name private for fear of being ridiculed. As I joke, I began referring to him as Neil deGrasse Sagan. After a few texts and phone calls back and forth, he said he would be happy to meet me. He had watched the viral video and had questions of his own for me.

Although he didn't believe a word of what happened to me, he was intrigued by my thoughts on time travel. He also shared some of my thoughts on whether or not a person sent back in time would be able to interact with their surroundings without changing the future. He was working on a book of his own on time travel and wanted to share his insights with me. He had read my books and said they were excellent science fiction but acknowledged that my understanding of the science behind time travel intrigued him.

I asked if he would meet for lunch at our friends' restaurant. He was willing, and since he lived in Philadelphia, he drove in the night before our lunch. He was cordial as we ate, sprinkling the initial conversation with his thoughts on my books. He had reread one of them the night before. He had also read Hayden's book the night before. It was released a few months ago.

Her book focused on a few of her time travel journeys, but she allowed me to sprinkle in some time travel jargon and concepts. Because her book involved her witnessing firsthand how prominent women in the Bible stood up to and overcame abuse, it was an instant bestseller. Even the folks who hated God and Christianity were instant lovers of her and her book. Her one book outsold all of my books a few weeks after it was published.

After lunch, Neil shared some lighthearted jokes about why he didn't believe my books could be true. The more we talked about it, the more serious the conversation got. Clearly, he had absolutely no interest in anything to do with God. It was as if he was insulted by the insinuation that God could move people through time. I made it clear to him that I was interested in the time travel aspect of our conversation and wasn't trying to convert him.

"I am not trying to get you to think like I think or believe like I believe," I stated. "I am really just trying to understand better how time travel works."

"Even though I am intrigued by your desire to understand time travel, I still don't understand why you claim that you actually traveled through time." Neil held up his hand to stop me from talking as he sipped his water.

"Nor do I understand why you claim your time travel book is true. If it were true, would you expect people to believe that God did it?"

I was going to respond, but I felt a slight familiar rumbling in my stomach. I knew the familiar rumbling was the predecessor to the Holy Spirit moving me through time, but why now? Why would He take me back in time now? And to when would He take me? I wondered if Neil would notice me glitch, but he was too wrapped up in what he was saying to notice anything.

"I mean, you mix the real potential of time travel with the ridiculous option that God exists, which we all know is..."

Neil didn't get to finish the sentence. I watched as Neil grabbed his stomach and gave me a weird look, and then we both disappeared.

We appeared on the same mountaintop where my journey initially started. I recognized it immediately. I also recognized the storm and the thunder as God spoke through the thunder to call my name and ask me questions. God had taken us back to my very first journey. I could hear God speaking through the thunder, asking me, "Who is it that darkens my plans with his ignorant words?"

Although I knew God was talking to the me that was back then, I also wondered whether God was speaking to Neil, who was with me now. I saw the me from back then, from my first journey, standing there confused as I, well, he, the me from back then, listened to God. I know this sounds confusing, but it's time travel. If I was confused, the me now, Neil had to be confused as well.

I turned and saw the look on Neil's face. He was confused but also scared as he stared at me, well, as he stared at the me from my first journey. As the thunder continued to boom and God spoke to me, the me from my first journey back then, through the thunder, Neil started shaking. He later told me he recognized the scene and what was happening from my book. He also couldn't deny that it was me, the me from back then, standing in front of him, as the me from now stood beside him.

"Is this...is this...?" he stuttered.

"Yes," I responded.

"And you...so you...?" he stuttered again.

"Were telling the truth? Yes," I responded again.

Neil's fear seemed to turn to excitement, probably at the thought that time travel existed and then at the understanding that he was experiencing it. But then we heard God speak to me again, well, to me back then. Then Neil's face flushed red, and he turned to me and grabbed both of my arms.

"Then...then God...God..."

"Is real," I said, finishing his sentence.

We both then felt the internal movement in our stomachs. I told Neil it was the Holy Spirit of God about to move us through time again.

"Unfortunately," I told Neil, "I don't think He is taking us home just yet."

"Oh, crap," Neil said. "Oh, crap. Oh, crap. Oh, crap."

For the record, Neil definitely did not use the word crap.

About The
Author

Floyd Hughes and his wife Christina live in Jefferson Hills, a suburb of Pittsburgh, where Floyd has served as pastor of CrossRoads Community Church of Jefferson Hills since 2007. He is co-host of multiple podcasts and an avid foodie and geek. One of his favorite things to do is to find creative ways to share the truths of God's Word with people in his circle of influence. He can be found on social media as @BigPhatPastor.

OTHER BOOKS BY THE AUTHOR:

It's About Time
Act Like an E-Christian
Hi My Name Is Jonah
Unwrapping Christ at Christmas
Evangelism: Easy as 1, 2, 3

BOOKS COMING SOON BY THE AUTHOR:

It's About Time Book 3: Let's Go Girls
It's About Time Book 4: When Darkness Falls